Hands off!

This book is for

GIRLS ONLY!

GIRLS ONLY!

All about periods and growing-up stuff

Vic Parker

Illustrations by Richard Williams

*Hodder
Children's
Books*

A division of Hachette Children's Books

Acknowledgements

With special thanks to consultant gynaecologist Dr Hilary McPherson of the Edinburgh Royal Infirmary for her invaluable expert advice.

Also huge thanks to Eileen Armstrong, Danielle, Maegan, Ashley, Rebecca and Victoria at Cramlington High School for reading and commenting on the manuscript.

And finally thank you to the many other girls – both young and grown-up – who helped in any way with the writing of this book.

About the author

Vic Parker is a writer of books for children and teenagers, who lives in Birmingham. She knows about young people because she also teaches dance and fitness classes to kids, and has a son and twenty-three young nieces and nephews – at the last count!

Contents

Introduction

Who would want to be a boy, when it's so great being a girl? Firstly, girls make the best friends. Together forever, you get to swap fab fashions, try out different hairstyles and muck about with make-up. Secondly, when you grow up, you can be whatever you want to be: vets, athletes, plumbers, models, designers, astronauts ... and mums too! Thirdly, girls are the best at lots of things. Some of the best popstars are girls (look at Madonna and Kylie), as are many of the best actresses (check out Cameron Diaz and Nicole Kidman), and many of the best writers (J K Rowling, Jacqueline Wilson and Anne Fine). Think of any famous, successful, gorgeous woman you like – she was once a girl just like you.

So what exactly happens to your body to turn you into a fab 'n' funky teenager and then into a grown-up babe? This book will tell you and your friends all about it. So check it out and get ready to be gorgeous.

Puzzled about periods?

Don't be!

Hands up if you've ever had a puppy or a kitten? If you have, you'll know how fast they grow and change into adult animals. These tiny bundles of fluff don't stay tiny bundles of fluff for long. From the day you bring your pet home, it takes only a few months before you realise that your puppy or kitten has grown up into a handsome hound or purr-fect puss – and you didn't even notice it was happening!

It's just the same with people. From the minute we are born, we are growing and changing all the time. And usually, we don't even notice that it's happening. For instance, you might only realise that you've grown a couple of centimetres taller when your best friend points out that your favourite jeans seem to have shrunk. But at certain times in our lives, we grow and change much faster than at others. A helpless, wriggling baby turns into a mischievous, giggling toddler after just 12 months!

Another time in our lives when we grow and change especially fast is between the ages of about nine and 17. This is when girls turn into glamorous babes and boys change into strapping hunks. Our bodies change so much in these few years that even the plainest, gawkiest girl in the class can blossom into a beautiful actress, and the skinniest, scrawniest boy can develop into an athletic football star.

Girltalk

66 My best friend Donna used to get called 'Spider' at school, because she was tall and skinny, with long gangly legs and arms. When she grew up, she became more beautiful than any of us – and she's now a part-time model. 99

Sue from Birmingham

Ready ... steady ... grow!

Many of the changes that take place between the ages of about nine and 17 happen on the outside of our bodies, where they're easy to spot. Boys start to sprout hair on their faces and have to buy razors. Girls begin to grow boobs and start wearing bras. Buying your first bra is a great opportunity to talk your mum or friends into some serious shopping.

However, other important changes start happening *inside* our bodies, so we don't realise that they are taking place. When these changes finally show, it can come as quite a surprise. They often seem to happen overnight. A boy might find one day that when he speaks, his voice is much deeper and richer than the day before. Or a girl might wake up to discover that she has started having periods.

What is a period?

A period is a very small amount of blood that comes out from between your legs for four to five days every month. DON'T PANIC! It may sound a bit scary, but it is nothing to worry about at all. *All* women are meant to have periods at the right time in their lives. That includes your mum, your friends' mums, your friends, your aunties and your teachers. It includes popstars, shop assistants, actresses, female doctors, sportswomen, TV presenters – even women vicars and nuns. It includes women who aren't married and women who are. Women who have had babies and women who haven't. Women in *every* country all over the world. So when you start having periods, you are in very good company. It is a sign that your body is working the right way.

Why do we have periods?

The biggest difference between young people and grown-ups is that girls and boys can't have babies together, but women and men can. It's the changes that take place in girls' and boys' bodies between the ages of about nine and 17 that make it possible for them to have babies together when they're grown-up. For girls, starting periods is the most important change. It means that your body is ready for you to have a baby one day … if you want one, that is. You certainly don't have to have one, just because you've started having periods. It's a choice that you can make when you're older.

7

Do boys have periods?

Nope. Men don't have periods. Boys change in other ways so they can have a baby with a woman when they are grown-up. Periods are special things for GIRLS ONLY!

How do you handle having a period?

There's no need for periods to be fussy or messy. Girls buy special pads to use from any supermarket or chemist. Most newsagents, late-night shops and petrol stations stock them too. The pads are shaped to fit inside your knickers comfortably and soak up the blood. They have a sticky strip underneath, so you can press them into your knickers and they stay in place securely. You can change the pad whenever you like. Just wrap it in some loo roll or the packet it came in and throw it into a bin.

How long do women have periods for?

Most women have a period about once every month until they are around 50 years old. Then they stop again. That is because by this age, women have either had babies or decided that they don't want them. They no longer need periods, so their bodies stop having them.

Why hasn't anyone told me about periods before?

Don't worry, having a period is not some big, mysterious secret. It's something that all grown-ups know about (yep, men too). All young people gradually find out how their body works as they grow up. Are you ready to find out more about yours?

You might feel a little embarrassed about periods at first – most girls do. So you can bet that your friends will all be feeling just like you. Don't forget that friends are great for talking things over and sharing things with. Also remember that your mum, your friends' mums, your aunties and older sisters, and your teachers all felt exactly the same way when they were your age. Now they talk with their friends quite openly about their periods. So it's a

9

good idea to speak about periods to a grown-up you trust. They'll be happy to tell you about their own experiences and answer all your questions.

Girltalk

" I thought my big sister might tease me when I asked her what having periods was like. Instead she told me all about it. She even showed me what pads she uses. It was the first time I'd ever seen one!" Emily from Belfast

TALK TIPS - tried and tested

So how do you bring the subject of periods into a conversation?

Here are some ideas to start you off ...

To get talking to your mum, auntie, or best friend's mum:

❀ You could wait until you're alone together, then ask her how old she was when she started having periods ...

❀ You could mention to her that you know an older girl who has just started her periods ... (It doesn't matter if you don't really. A little fib like this is OK if it helps you get going.)

❀ When you're out shopping together, you could ask her to show you where the period pad section is, so you can see what they look like ...

If you live with someone you find it harder to talk to about things like this, such as your dad or a foster-parent:

❀ You could add period pads to the shopping list, which will let them know you're thinking about periods.

❀ You could leave a copy of this book somewhere they're bound to see it. They're sure to ask what you think of it!

To get talking to an older sister or your friends:

❀ You could wait until you see a period pad advert on TV or in a magazine, and then say, "What do you think it's like to use one of those?"

❀ You could suggest that you go to the local library to get out some good stories. Then when you're there say, "I wonder where the books on starting periods are ..."

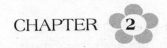

CHAPTER 2

Be clued up ...

All your questions answered

As you grow up, you're bound to wonder whether the changes happening to your body are normal. Everyone worries from time to time – yep, boys too. The main thing to remember is that *it's normal to be different*. After all, we're all different heights and weights, and we all have different skin, eye and hair colour. We all have different talents – from shooting netball hoops, to working out maths problems, to drawing fab cartoons, to being the greatest friend. And we all have different likes and dislikes. So it follows that everyone's periods will be different too.

Here are the answers to some questions about periods that are often asked by girls just like you ...

How old are you when you get your first period?

There is no set age for girls to start having periods. Most girls have their first period some time between the ages of 11 and 14. However, some girls start as early as eight or nine, and some girls don't start until they are 16 or 17.

There is no point worrying about when you will get your first period. There is nothing you can do to make yourself start earlier or to put it off till later. It will happen whenever your body is ready.

However, your body might give you some clues that will help you guess when you might start. You almost certainly won't start your periods until a year or two after you have begun to grow boobs, and when soft hair has started to appear between your legs and under your arms. Another clue is that a small amount of wet, sticky stuff called mucus might come from between your legs, leaving whitish stains in your knickers. This is perfectly normal and nothing to worry about. So until you notice these things, you probably have quite a long time to wait until you start having periods.

Girltalk

“ I started my periods at
the same age as my mum started hers.
So did my friend, Vanessa. But it's not like
that for everybody. You'll have to
wait and see! **”**

Helen from London

I've heard my older sister talk about 'coming on'. Does she mean getting her period?

Ten out of ten! Many girls say they are "on" when they have their period, but there are lots of other slang names for it too, such as: on the rag, having the curse, on the blob, and having the painters in.

What does a period look like?

Do you usually think URRRRRRGH! at the sight of blood? Well, don't worry if you're squeamish. When you have a period, you lose only about four to six tablespoons of blood altogether – and it flows out over four or five days. In any case, period blood often doesn't look like the blood you see when you cut yourself. The flow at the start and end of your period is often quite thick and a brownish-colour – not much like usual bleeding at all.

Does it hurt when you have a period?

Many girls get some tummy-ache when their period starts. This is actually quite useful, because it tells you when it's time to go to the loo and stick a period pad in your knickers. However, you might come across a big-mouth who tries to show off by telling you that she's already started her periods and it's *really really* painful. She's just trying to get you worried. Grown-ups like your mum get rid of period pain by taking one or two headache tablets. (See pages 34–36 for more info.)

Does having a period mean that I'm ill?

Usually when you bleed, it's because you've had an accident and fallen over or cut yourself. (Hopefully not in front of any gorgeous boys!) However, when you have a period, it's not because you're injured or ill – it's because you're healthy. Period blood means that your body is working as it should. It tells you that you are growing up just right.

You only lose a very small amount of blood when you have your period, though it might look or feel like more than this, and some girls lose more than others. So having a period will not make you weak or ill. For instance, you are not more likely to catch a cold during your period than at any other time during the month.

However, in order to make blood, everyone's body needs the iron found in green vegetables, breakfast cereals and red meat. So make sure you eat plenty of these foods to stay strong and healthy. (You don't have to eat red meat if you're vegetarian. To make up for it, have leafy green salads of spinach and watercress, experiment with tasty recipes that include lentils and beans, munch on bread and cereals that are based on whole grains, and snack on dried apricots – they're all full of iron.) If you're doing all of this and you still feel under the weather then visit your doctor or school nurse who will be able to advise you.

Does having a period mean that I'm dirty?

Having your period does not mean that you are dirty, either. If you change your period pad every few hours and wash, shower or bath as usual, you'll stay as fresh as a daisy.

How can you take a shower or bath if blood is coming out?

There is no problem with taking off your knickers and period pad for a short time to have a shower. And when you lie in a bath, the pressure of the water stops your period flowing for a while anyway. Before you get into the shower or bath, just go to the loo and wipe yourself well with loo paper. Then you won't notice any blood, even when you wash between your legs. Get a wodge of loo paper ready

for drying between your legs when you get out.
Don't forget a big fluffy towel for the rest of you.
Make sure you have your knickers and a fresh
period pad ready to put on straight away, and
you're fixed.

How long does a period last?

Most girls have periods that last four to five days.
However, some girls' periods last just two to three
days. Other girls have periods that last for six to
seven days. Remember, it's normal to be different. It
might also very from month to month, particularly
when you start having periods.

My friend says that her sister doesn't
use period pads, she uses tampons.
What are they?

A tampon is a roll of cotton wool the size and
shape of a lipstick or mascara. Instead of sticking a
tampon to your knickers, you slip it inside your
body where the blood comes out. This doesn't hurt
at all, and when a tampon is in place, you can't
even feel it is there. It works by soaking up the
blood before it leaves your body. When you want to
take it out, you just pull on a little string and it
glides out. So you can change a tampon easily and
regularly, just like you do with regular period pads.

Most girls start off with period pads and wait till later to try tampons, because period pads are easier to start with. But if you want to try tampons as soon as you start having periods, then that's fine. Some girls ask their mums or older sisters to show them what to do, and every pack of tampons comes with clear instructions. On the other hand, if you don't like the sound of tampons, you don't ever have to use one. It's entirely up to you.

Girltalk

66 I got my first period right in the middle of a dancing competition. I was worried that the shape of a period pad might show through my leotard when I was on stage. But my best friend, Anna, told me to try tampons straight away because she'd used them right from the start and hadn't found them difficult at all. She even came into the loo with me and helped me sort myself out. She's such a good friend – we share absolutely everything together. 99

Lucy from Hertfordshire

Can you tell when someone is having their period?

Next time you're in a shopping centre or on the bus, look at all the girls and women around you. Can you tell who's having their period and who isn't? No – but a lot of them will be. There is no way that you can tell just by looking at someone if they are having their period. It is impossible to see someone wearing a tampon, and period pads are made so thin, light and close-fitting that they're extremely difficult to spot – even if a girl is wearing tight jeans.

In any case, having your period is nothing you should feel you have to hide or be embarrassed about. Pick any day in the month – out of all the women in the world aged between 10 and 50, a quarter will be having their period. Having a period is a totally natural thing for girls. It's just as natural as having to wee, and *everyone* has to do that, don't they?

FAB FACT or RUBBISH RUMOUR?

See if you can guess whether the following sentences are true or false ...

1. You can't wash your hair when you have a period.

2. Blood just gushes out when you have a period.

3. Some female animals have periods too.

4. Periods are smelly.

5. There are things you can do to prevent yourself from starting periods.

6. In some parts of the world, female family members and friends have a celebration when a girl gets her first period.

Answers

1. *False*
   There is no reason at all why you shouldn't wash your hair or shower or take a bath during your period, just the same as normal.

2. *False*
   If your period is heavy, you may feel a gush of blood, which often seems to be more than it

actually is. In general, period blood flows out over four or five days, and not all at once.

3. *True*
Some female animals, such as dogs, have a sort of period called "a season" – although you might not even notice any blood coming from them.

4. *False*
Period blood is not smelly or dirty. As long as you change your period pad regularly, you will stay your clean, sweet-smelling self!

5. *False*
There is nothing you can do to prevent yourself starting periods, and there's nothing you can do to make them come earlier, either. Your body will start in its own good time, when it's ready.

6. *True*
Some mums in America hold fun parties for their daughters when they get their first period. Parents in many other countries and cultures mark the event in special ways. Getting your first period is something to be proud of, not ashamed of in any way.

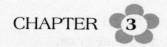
Be prepared ...

Know just what to do

Have you ever had a good look inside your mum's or auntie's handbag? Along with the usual purse, keys, lipstick, mirror, notepad, pen and sweets, you will usually find a small, flat, square thing in a prettily patterned plastic wrapper. Guess what this is? Tissues? Nope. Spare tights? Nope. Try again ... Yep – you got it! It's a period pad. You might also find a plastic-wrapped tampon or a tampon holder that looks like a lipstick or glasses case.

When you think you've reached the age when you might get your first period, you may want to start doing the same thing. It's no trouble to slip a period pad inside your school backpack or gym bag. It's also a good excuse to take your best friend shopping so you can both choose funky little bags for discos and parties. After all, your period can start at any time of the day or night, so you can't tell where you'll be. If you're not at home, you might be having a sleepover at your friend's house, or at school, or at the shops, or at a dance class. So like they tell boys at Scouts, it's best to, "Be prepared!"

The perfect pad

You can always ask your mum, big sister or an older friend to buy your first period pads for you. Or you might want to take them shopping with you, so they can help you buy your own. There are a lot of period pads to choose from. Some are different shapes, some have sticky 'wings' to press around the sides of your knickers as well as a sticky strip underneath, and some are thicker than others. Night-time pads are thick enough to give you extra protection while you're asleep, and "panty liners" are especially thin so you can wear them when your period is due – just in case. Shops usually call period pads "sanitary towels" or "sanitary protection".

When you go up to pay, don't be put off if the checkout assistant is a man, not a woman. There's no need to be embarrassed. Over half the people in the world are women, and they buy period pads in shops every day. So men who work on checkouts won't even bat an eyelid.

What to do when you get your first period

Sooner or later, the big day will come – the day
when you get your first period. It may not look like
blood to start off with. You might just notice brown
stains in your pyjamas or knickers. You're clearly a
clever sort of person because you're reading this
book, so you'll probably be well prepared with a
period pad in your bag. Just go into the nearest loo,
press it into your knickers, and away you go.

It's important to tell one or two older people who are closest to you, like your parents or carers or sisters. Firstly, they're useful to talk things over with. Secondly, they will be really proud for you. After all, it is a very important day in your life. Your body is telling you that you have taken a big step towards becoming grown-up and glamorous.

What to do if you're not ready

Let's imagine for a moment that you've been unlucky. Your first period has started on the day when you're not carrying any of your bags with a period pad in. What should you do? Most importantly,

❀ Don't panic ❀

Tell your mum, or your friend's mum, or another older person you trust, like your favourite teacher, school nurse, classroom assistant or school secretary straight away. They will help you get sorted out quickly and easily – don't forget, they will have been doing it themselves for a long time. Older girls often carry an emergency supply of pads in their bag too, so don't be afraid to ask.

What about if you're not with anyone you feel you can tell? Well, still

🌼 Don't panic 🌼

Wherever there are people, there are loos somewhere nearby. And in most public ladies' loos there is a machine on the wall which sells period pads (sometimes tampons too). They come in packs of one or two, made specially for emergencies, and they don't cost much.

So what if you're not with anyone you feel you can tell, *and* you haven't got any spare change for the machine in the ladies' loos. What do you do? Well, you still

✿ Don't panic ✿

In an emergency like this, fold some loo paper into a wodge and put that in your knickers. No one will know if you don't tell them, and it will do the job until you *are* with someone you can ask to help you out.

Now you'll be able to cope in any situation, so there's no need to worry, is there?

Quick change

At the start of your period, the flow of blood is often heaviest. It usually gets lighter as it goes on. So for the first day or two, you might want to change your pad every couple of hours or so. Towards the end of your period, you might need to change your pad only two or three times a day. Some girls like to change their pad whenever they go to the loo. But you don't necessarily have to do this if you still feel dry and clean.

Don't feel that you have to think up cunning ways to smuggle a period pad secretly into the loo. Women like your mum always take their handbags into the loo with them. So do the same. Take your schoolbag, gym bag or handbag with you when you go for a wee. That way, no one will ever know if you're changing a period pad or not. Smart, eh?

Night-night, sleep tight

Some girls and women find that their period, usually starts during the night. No one knows exactly why this is – it's one of those crazy things that just happens. So if you wake up to find spots of blood on your nightie or the sheet, don't be alarmed. Pull on some knickers and a period pad and go back to sleep, then put anything dirty straight into the wash in the morning. Once you've had your period a few times you'll be able to predict roughly when you might get your period, so you can wear a period pad in bed just in case.

You'll have to wear knickers and a period pad in bed for the four or five nights that your period lasts. However, you may notice that less blood flows out at night compared to the daytime. This isn't because of some complicated medical reason. It's simply because you're lying down instead of standing or sitting up.

Bye-bye, period pain

As you know, when you get your period it might give you a tummy-ache. It's usually quite low down in your stomach and isn't too bad. But sometimes, it might spread to your back and your knees and make you feel quite fed up. This is called period pain. Occasionally on the first day of your period, it might be bad enough to make you feel a bit faint and need to lie down.

If you get period pain, there are several ways you can get rid of it. Doing some exercise should help, so why not put on one of your favourite CDs and groove in your room with your friends? If you don't feel like that, you could always curl up on the sofa with a hot-water bottle on your tummy, or special sticky heat patches that you can get from chemists and some supermarkets. If these things

don't work, then ask a grown-up for one or two of the mild painkillers that they use for headaches. They will nearly always do the trick – so there's usually no need for a period to be painful for very long. There might be a very rare occasion when painkillers don't make you feel better. If this happens, NEVER take more than the recommended dose on the packet. Go and tell a trusted grown-up, such as a parent, friend's parent, teacher or school nurse. They will know what to do and will take you to see a doctor if needs be, who will definitely be able to help. So there's no need to suffer in silence.

Getting out of bed on the wrong side ...

Have you ever noticed that your mum or older sister sometimes seem to be grumpy and irritable for no reason at all? Chances are that she's expecting her period. This is because in the few days just before your period starts, the changes going on in your body can make you feel like shouting at people and bashing them over the head even though they've done nothing to upset you. You might also feel really weepy – as if you'd just watched *Titanic*!

Feeling like this is not the same as just being moody. In fact, it has a special scientific name: PMT (premenstrual tension) or PMS (premenstrual syndrome). Some girls never get PMT at all. Others find that it strikes them some months and not others, while a few girls get PMT before their period every month as regular as clockwork. Taking daily tablets of vitamin B6 or evening primrose oil can really help to get rid of the symptoms. Steering clear of chocolate, coffee, tea and fizzy drinks can also help to keep you feeling like your usual chirpy self all month long. However, next time you notice your mum or older sister slamming doors in a temper or sniffling their way through an economy-sized box of tissues, try to be especially nice and thoughtful to them. Now you know that they probably have a very good reason for it.

Can I still do sports and swim when I'm having my period?

There's no reason why you can't do all your usual activities when you have your period, whether it's horseriding, ice-skating, ballet dancing or karate.

37

In fact, as you've just read, doing some exercise is often good for getting rid of tummy-ache. Just wear a period pad or a tampon, and you're all set.

You can even swim, if you want to. The only thing is that it's not a good idea to wear a period pad inside a swimming costume as it will just get soggy. As long as you're not going to hang about in the changing rooms or on the poolside, you'll be fine without a period pad while you swim. If you feel this is a bit risky and you don't want to spoil your time in the pool worrying about your period, the best thing to do whilst swimming is to wear a tampon. However if you have a swimming lesson and you don't want to do either of these just tell your teacher that you don't want to swim as you've got your period.

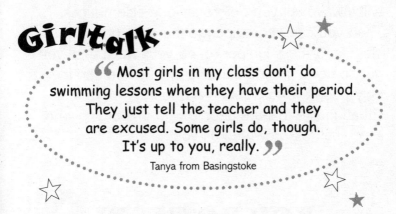

Girltalk

66 Most girls in my class don't do swimming lessons when they have their period. They just tell the teacher and they are excused. Some girls do, though. It's up to you, really. 99

Tanya from Basingstoke

Period fashion

There are no special clothes to wear or not to wear while you are having a period. You can still put on whatever you like – even tight jeans or short mini-skirts. However, some girls like to wear dark-coloured knickers and clothes on the first couple of days of their period. This is just in case a spot or two of blood leaks out of your knickers and on to your clothes. An accident like this hardly ever happens. But if it does, it is much less likely to show up on dark clothes than on light clothes. So by sticking to dark clothes, you can relax and enjoy whatever you are doing, without trying to check your back view in a mirror all the time.

If the worst comes to the absolute worst and you *do* have an accident that shows up, a true friend will always tell you before anyone else notices. Then you can either sponge the stain off your clothes, or tie a jumper round your waist until you get somewhere you can change. Remember, the only people who would make fun of you in a situation like this are people with tiny brains who aren't half as grown-up as you.

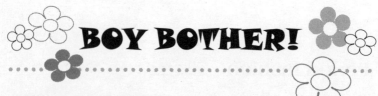

BOY BOTHER!

Can't boys be a right pain sometimes?!

If you have a brother, you'll know that they think it's funny to do things like burst into your bedroom when you're not expecting it. If you're faced with boys at school, you'll know how annoying it can be when they gang up together to tease you about something. Well, when boys find out about periods, they often start being really irritating by trying to make a joke out of them. For instance, they might ask you whether you've started yet, just to try to embarrass you and get on your nerves.

If you do run into any bother with boys about things to do with periods, here's how to stay cool and deal with it. It will soon be the boys who are scarpering red-faced, not you and your friends.

Plan A:
The first thing to do is to ignore them. This is by far the best plan. If you let boys see that their teasing is working and that you're getting flustered, it will just egg them on to try to wind you up even more. Just grab a friend and walk off together, talking loudly about something completely different.

Plan B:

If you really feel as if you're going to explode if you don't say something back, you could try: "It's a shame that *you're* not showing any sign of growing up yet, isn't it?" If that doesn't send them running, you could add: "Maybe you'll *never* grow up, and you'll be stuck as morons forever!" If this fails, you'll have to resort to desperate measures. Try saying, "Hasn't anybody told you what happens to boys' bodies if they talk too much about periods?" Then look straight at their trouser area, pull a disgusted face, and make a tutting sound, as if something *seriously* nasty might happen to them down below. The boys will say, "No, what happens?" Which is when you reply, "I *can't believe* that you don't know! But trust me, you really wouldn't want to find out. So I'd stop banging on about periods, if I were you." Then walk off, cool as a cucumber. (Of course, nothing at all really happens to boys if they talk about periods. But *they* won't know that, will they?)

Plan C:

If neither Plan A nor Plan B work, you're obviously up against the most aggravating boys in the universe. Time for Plan C. This is where you and your best friend go to see a teacher at a quiet moment. Tell your teacher that some boys are bothering you by being silly about periods. Ask if your teacher could give a talk to everyone about the changes that happen to both girls and boys as they grow up. The boys will probably find this much more embarrassing than you and your friends, and won't want to mention things like periods ever again!

CHAPTER 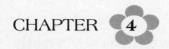 4

Be smart ...

Surprise your science teacher!

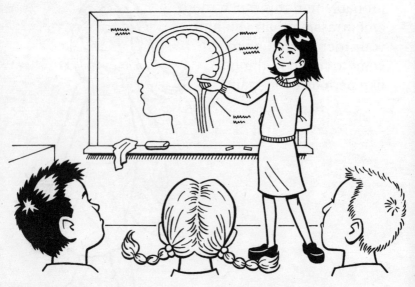

By now, you're probably wondering exactly what happens inside your body to make you have a period. Ready to find out? Put on your thinking cap and you'll soon be ready to show off to your friends and stun your teachers.

Inside your insides

Everyone has the same tubes and organs for digesting and absorbing food. But girls and boys have a different set of tubes and organs for making babies. Girls' special insides look like this:

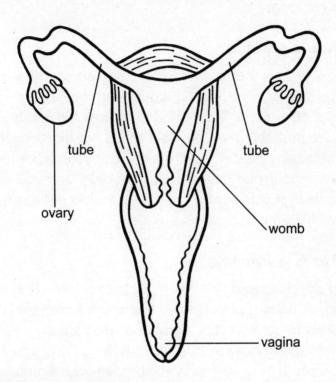

What is an ovary?

An ovary is a little pod filled with hundreds of teeny-tiny eggs. Every egg is only the size of the tip of a needle.

What is a tube?

In the drawing on page 45 the tubes look much thicker and longer than they really are. In real life, they are very thin – a bit like a strand of spaghetti. In fully-grown women, each tube is only about 10 cm long.

What is a womb?

The womb is the space inside a woman where a baby grows. If you tighten your hand into a clenched fist, you'll get an idea of how big it is … You're probably thinking, "But that's not big enough to fit a baby inside!" You're right. But your womb is elastic. So if one day when you're older and you decide that you want a baby, your womb will easily stretch as the baby grows bigger.

What is a vagina?

You say this word like this: "vadge-eye-nuh". This is a small, narrow passageway that leads from your insides to outside your body. It is what a baby travels through when it is being born … Yep, you guessed it! Your vagina is elastic, like your womb. So when a woman is having a baby, it can stretch much bigger than usual, to let the baby through.

The entrance to your vagina is a hole between your legs. It is in between the hole where you wee (near the front of your body) and the hole where you poo (your bottom). You might not even have noticed it before.

You have had all this amazing equipment inside you ever since you were born. However, it only starts working when your body is ready to have periods.

What happens inside you when you have a period?

When you're the right age to start having periods, your body tells one of the ovaries to release just one egg. The egg is picked up and travels into the nearest tube. Then it carries on moving down into your womb. When the egg gets there, and it isn't the right time to have a baby, the lining of your womb melts away. This means that blood flows through your vagina for four or five days, giving you a period. It flushes the egg out with it. It's far too tiny to see.

All this happens very, very slowly. In fact, the whole thing takes about a month. As soon as your period finishes, your body starts getting ready to release another egg all over again. This is why girls get periods about once every month.

Your personal pattern

After you have your first period, you might find that you miss a month or two before you have another one. You might also discover that you have a shorter period one month and a longer period the next month. Or, one particular month, you might notice that your period stops after a day or two and then starts again. It is quite normal for girls to have irregular periods for the first few months. As the months go on, all these sort of changes usually settle down into a regular pattern.

The pattern for most girls is that they get a period every 28 days. This means that if they count the first day of their period as Day 1, they will count up to Day 28, and then the following day their next period will start. (They count this as Day 1 again.)

Most girls keep count of the days by marking them in their diary or on a calendar, like this.

JULY

S	M	T	W	T	F	S
				1	2	3
4	5	6	7	8	9	10
11	12	*day 1* (13)	**2** 14	**3** 15	**4** 16	**5** 17
6 18	**7** 19	**8** 20	**9** 21	**10** 22	**11** 23	**12** 24
13 25	**14** 26	**15** 27	**16** 28	**17** 29	**18** 30	**19** 31

SEPTEMBER

S	M	T	W	T
			1	2
5	6	7	8	9
12	13	14	15	16
19	20	21	22	23
26	27	28	29	30

AUGUST

S	M	T	W	T	F	S
20 1	**21** 2	**22** 3	**23** 4	**24** 5	**25** 6	**26** 7
27 8	**28** 9	*day 1* (10)	**2** 11	**3** 12	**4** 13	**5** 14
6 15	**7** 16	**8** 17	**9** 18	**10** 19	**11** 20	**12** 21
13 22	**14** 23	**15** 24	**16** 25	**17** 26	**18** 27	**19** 28
20 29	**21** 30	**22** 31				

OCTOBER

S	M	T	W	T
3	4	5	6	7
10	11	12	13	14
17	18	19	20	21
24	25	26	27	28
31				

But remember – it's normal to be different. Many girls settle into shorter or longer patterns than 28 days. Some girls may have a period every 24 days, or less. Other girls may have a period every 32 days, or more. And some girls never settle into a regular pattern at all. Your body will decide for itself.

Doctors have a special name for your personal pattern of monthly periods. They call it your menstrual cycle. (You say "men-stroo-al" cycle.) By the way, "cycle" has nothing to do with bicycles. Doctors and science teachers use the word "cycle" when they mean that something happens over and over again.

Girltalk

66 My best friends and I all started off having our periods at different times in the month. But after a year or so, we were all coming on together the same week. My friend Susie told her mum who said that sometimes this happens to best friends. Because we're such close friends, our bodies start working closely together too. No one knows exactly how it happens, but it's wicked, isn't it? 99

Gail from Glasgow

Do periods sometimes stop?

You might remember from earlier on in the book that women stop having periods at around the age of 50. And you've just read that when you first start having periods, you might miss a month or two. This is perfectly usual and nothing at all to worry about. There are a few other reasons why girls sometimes stop having periods.

Many girls worry a lot about their weight. They think that they are fat, even if they are slim. So they go on diets and stop eating lots of things, in order to make themselves thinner. This is not healthy for your body at all (or for grown-ups, for that matter). It can make you very poorly in lots of ways, including stopping your periods. If you are at all worried about your weight, talk it over with your mum, auntie, favourite teacher, doctor or school nurse. They will know what to do to help you, without you making yourself ill. If you notice that a friend keeps skipping meals or talks a lot about being on a diet it's very important to tell an adult. They will take you seriously and you're definitely *not* wasting their time.

Your periods can also sometimes stop if you are very stressed out. For instance, you might be worked up about exams at school. Or maybe people are rowing a lot at home and it's making you upset. If this happens, it's best to share your worries with someone older that you trust. Older people have been through these kind of things themselves and they will understand how you feel. Even if there's nothing you can actually do to sort the problem out, just sharing it with someone can make you feel much, much better. Telling them that your periods have stopped will help you stop worrying about that, too. If you can talk to someone in your family then that's great. If you can't, why not try someone like your best friend's mum, or your doctor or school nurse.

Girls who do a lot of training for sport or dance sometimes stop having periods too. It doesn't usually happen if you go to gym club or athletics

or ballet class two or three times a week. But if you are in a special training programme for big competitions that involves working-out every day, you might find that you start to miss periods. If this happens, it means that you are working your body too hard or not eating the right food to cope with all your training. So you should tell your parents or your coach. They can then help you eat the right things or change your training programme, so that your body gets back into tip-top form. After all, to win those competitions you need to be in great shape all-round, don't you?

There is one other reason why women stop having periods. This is if they are expecting a baby. So how does this happen? Just read on …

Having a baby

Boys do not grow eggs inside their tummies. Instead, they make thousands of tadpole-like things called sperm. Each sperm is even smaller than one of your teeny-tiny eggs. If you could make a sperm and egg much bigger so you could see them, they would look a bit like this.

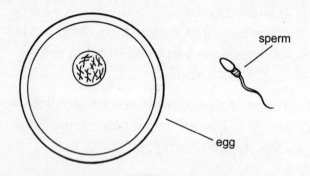

sperm

egg

When you are older, you might settle down with someone you really love and both decide that you want to have a baby. When a woman and a man feel like this they make love, which is also called having sex. In a special cuddle, the man's sperm go into the woman's vagina. Afterwards, the sperm travel into the woman's womb and up into the tubes. It doesn't hurt or anything. The woman can't feel it happening at all – sperm are much too tiny for that. If a sperm meets an egg and joins up with it, it will grow into a baby. When this happens, the womb lining does not melt away. The lining of the womb is there to protect and nourish the egg. This is why, when a woman is expecting a baby, she does not have periods.

It's important to remember that an egg can *never* grow into a baby on its own. So starting periods does *not* mean that you might have a baby when you don't want to. The only way you can have a baby is if you have sex with a boy. And most girls decide that they don't want a baby until they're proper grown-ups like your mum and are sure that they really want to.

LET'S TALK ABOUT SEX

Lots of girls and boys don't much like thinking about how sex works. This is because it can seem like quite a strange, scary thing until you're older and you've met someone that you really love. So if thinking about sex bothers you, don't worry about it. Just put it to the back of your mind. It's great that you know about it, but you are not going to have to do anything else about it for a while, until you feel ready and happy.

Other girls have lots of questions about sex that they want to know the answers to straight away. Just like periods, sex is not a big mysterious secret. It is not rude or naughty to want to find out about it – it is a perfectly normal part of growing-up. So if you feel curious, here are some ways you can learn more:

🌼 You could start a conversation with your mum or dad with: "I've started thinking about how babies are made and was wondering if you could tell me about it?"

🌼 If you don't want to talk to an older person at home, you might find it easier to speak to your school nurse, counsellor or support assistant. Say to her, "I'd like to ask you about something private. Could I meet up with you somewhere quiet at break or lunchtime, please?" Then when you get together, you can explain that you've started wondering how babies are made and was hoping that she could explain. They will be very glad that you've asked, and won't mind if you take a friend along with you for support.

There are lots of books you can borrow from the library about how babies are made. Don't be scared to ask a librarian – that's what they're there for. Books usually have pictures and diagrams to help explain tricky words and new ideas. It's a good thing to ask an older person you trust to help choose them for you (like your mum, your auntie or your best friend's mum). This is because they will be able to pick the right books for your age group. After all, it's no fun reading a book that's too easy or too difficult, is it?

A few girls and boys have questions about sex because the way a grown-up is behaving with them or touching them makes them feel extremely uncomfortable. If this is happening to you, it's really important that you tell another grown-up what is happening and how bad it makes you feel. Then they will be able to help you or put your mind at rest, and you will soon be feeling much happier.

Finally, don't believe everything you hear older girls or boys saying about sex. Just because they're bigger than you doesn't mean that they always know better than you. People sometimes make mistakes, or even deliberately pass round silly stories because they think it's naughty and fun. So if you hear something and you're not sure whether it's right or wrong, don't be afraid to ask a grown-up you trust. Then you can be really cool and put everybody straight.

Girltalk

66 My mum told me about periods and sex when I was having a day off school with a cold. At first I thought it all sounded really yucky – but later I started to feel quite proud that I knew the real way that babies are made. 99

Nadia from London

59

The scientific bit

Doctors and science teachers use special words for having periods and for the bits and pieces inside your body. Here is a list of some of them.

Common name	Proper medical name
having your period	**menstruation** [you say "men-stroo-ay-shun"]
ovary	**ovary** [you say "oh-va-ree']
egg	**ovum** [you say "oh-vum"]
tube	**Fallopian tube** [you say "fal-oh-pee-un" tube]
vagina	**vagina** [you say "vadge-eye-nuh"]
womb	**uterus** [you say "yoo-tur-us"]
your period pattern	**menstrual cycle** [you say "men-stroo-al" cycle]
having sex	**sexual intercourse** [you say "sex-yoo-al in-ter-course"]
sperm	**sperm** [you say "spurm"]
expecting a baby	**being pregnant**
missing a period (when you're not expecting a baby)	**amenorrhoea** [you say "ay-men-or-ee-uh"]

No one really uses these medical words when they're talking to their family or friends. But your science teacher and your doctor will think you're a pretty smart cookie if you know them anyway.

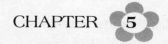

CHAPTER 5

Be gorgeous ...

Have a beautiful bod

The years just before and after you start having periods are called puberty. Puberty just means "changing into a grown-up". Boys go through puberty too. However, their bodies start to change a couple of years later than girls'. You will notice this when you move to secondary school, after you have been there for about a year. You and your friends will suddenly start to grow taller, leaving the boys in your class behind. A couple of years later, it will be their turn. They will soon catch you up! By the time you all leave school for good, most of you will have reached the height you will stay for the rest of your lives.

Zapping zits

So what other changes happen to your body as you grow up? Well, even the coolest teenagers get spots sometimes. This doesn't mean that you have dirty skin. It's just that all the changes going on inside you sometimes unbalance your body. So you might break out in pimples on your face, back or chest – especially around the time of your period.

The bad news is that *everyone* gets spots from time to time – even top models and actresses. The good news is that they know lots of top tips for dealing with the problem which helps to keep their skin looking sensational.

STAR SKIN-CARE SECRETS

Drink lots of plain water every day – at least six glasses. That may sound a lot, but it's only two glasses each at breakfast, lunch and teatime. Look at pictures of your favourite celebs in magazines and you'll often see they're carrying a bottle of water or have one sticking out of their bag. Now you know why.

Eat plenty of fresh fruit and vegetables. They're *much* better for giving your skin a healthy glow than crisps, chips, chocolate and fizzy drinks. If you think apples, oranges and pears are boring, look out for more unusual fruits next time you're at the supermarket. Mangoes, papayas and lychees all make great snacks. And if you think veg means boiled sprouts and cabbage, think again. There are lots of crisp, delicious salads you can rustle up, with a spoonful of spicy dressing. And your skin will thank you for it …

✿ All models, actresses and popstars know that when you get a spot, you should leave it alone. Don't be tempted to squeeze it, or it might leave a tiny scar when it heals. You can buy special creams from any chemist which will help spots clear up fast.

✿ If you look closely at the pictures in magazines, you'll see that most celebs don't wear make-up when they're not working. They say that they "like to let their skin breathe" by not clogging it up with foundations and powders. But stars always have a concealer stick or cream handy – just for emergencies. Then if a dreaded spot breaks out right on the day of an important party, they can just cover it up.

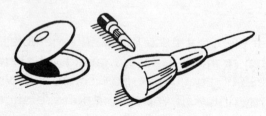

✿ All gorgeous girls also pay attention to keeping their skin clean. They wash their hands a lot, so that they don't carry germs on their fingers when they touch their face. You don't need to buy expensive, hi-tech lotions and potions for cleaning your face; in fact many celebs swear by soap and water. Other stars and make-up artists think that simple, cheap products are the best. They often like to use wipes and creams made for babies, because they're so light and gentle. The most important thing is to find out what is right for your particular type of skin. If you just have the odd pimple now and again, a soap-free facial wash or cleansing lotion might be all you need for peachy-perfect skin. If you're unlucky and develop problem skin most of the time, you might find that a medicated facial wash gives you the best results. There are also some fantastic medicines that can clear up bad outbreaks of spots that won't go away by themselves. Just ask your doctor, who will be happy to advise you.

Hair flair

Let's face it, we all want healthy, shiny hair. From this point of view, growing up can be a bit of a bummer, because you might find that your hair starts to get greasy. Rest assured that it won't stay like this forever. After a year or two, you'll return to the luscious locks you have now.

In the meantime, if your hair does start getting a bit dull and lank, it's a great excuse to have lots of fun playing about with it to make it look good. The first thing to try is changing your usual shampoo for one especially for greasy hair. Next, if your hair still looks rather flat and lifeless when it's down, get together with your friends and experiment with some exciting up-dos. You could try braids, French plaits, top-knots, or simply two or three ponytails. And just think about all the fantastic clips, grips, elastics, scrunchies and hairbands you can use. Not to mention hair wraps and beads. Fixing your hair neatly and tidily with colourful, sparkly things will help to draw attention away from your limp locks. Everyone will be admiring your fab hair decoration instead.

Finally, if you get really fed up with your hair, it's the perfect time to visit the salon to try out a dramatic new style. The stars change their haircuts all the time because they know how great a fab new look can make you feel. Flick through some magazines for ideas. You don't want anything that will take too long to sort out in the morning – after all, we all need our beauty sleep! If your hair is long and all one-length, a shoulder-length or chin-length bob can work wonders. You'll still look like you've got long hair, but you'll be amazed at the chic and trendy new you. Going for an even shorter, choppier style can look seriously cool and funky too – and will be dead easy to look after.

Girltalk

66 My big sister is a trainee in a hairdresser's and one night she asked if I wanted her to give me a new style. I was a bit nervous 'cos I knew she hadn't had much practice, but she said she'd just shape the back and put in some long layers round the front. My friends thought it looked great – really grown-up. 99

Lara from Leeds

Shaping up

As you go through the years of being a teenager, your body will slowly change shape until you look much more like the curvy women who model in magazines for older girls.

The first thing you might notice is that you start to grow boobs. There's no set age for this to start happening. It can start at 11 or younger, or it may not begin until 16 or so. Don't worry, you won't go from being flat-chested to looking like Barbie overnight. Your boobs will develop slowly over several years. When your boobs do start to grow, they might feel a little tender at first. Sometimes, one grows a bit faster than the other, too. Don't worry – all this is perfectly normal. They will even out and settle down in the end.

Because girls' boobs grow at different times, you might feel embarrassed if yours start early, or left behind if yours start late. Just remember: it's normal to be different. Boys can also have an annoying habit of pointing out your new boobs and making jokes about bras. Do your very best just to ignore them. In any case, nature will get its own back for you. A couple of years after your chest begins to grow bigger, the boys in your class will find that their willies start to grow bigger.

They'll soon be far too worried about what's happening to their own bodies to notice what's happening to yours!

Another change that happens over time is that your hips will get wider, so that your bum gets fuller too. This does *not* mean that you are getting fat. It just means that you're becoming a gorgeous babe. In fact, wider hips mean that your waist looks slimmer and sexier, so you'll look even more gorgeous wearing crop tops than you do now. Any boys who might have been teasing you will soon be eating their words and start to fancy you instead.

You might hear older girls moaning that their boobs are too small or their bums are too big. This is not because there is a perfect size and shape that everybody should be aiming for. There isn't. In fact, fashions change. For instance, one year, flat chests are in, the next year, everyone is admiring big boobs. The truth is that everybody always wants what they haven't got. For example, if you've got straight black hair, you've probably always longed for blonde curls. If you've got blue eyes, you've probably always admired your friend's brown ones. If you're tall, you've probably always wanted to be a bit smaller. Well, girls are just the same with the size and shape of their bum and boobs. So whatever size yours end up, try to be happy with what you've got. Even if you don't like them, there are sure to be loads of other girls who think they're great and wish that theirs were just like yours.

Girltalk

66 I was the first girl in my class to start wearing a bra. I used to get really embarrassed about changing for PE because I felt like everyone was looking at me. But a few months later most of my friends needed bras too. 99

Shaheena from Manchester

Fit 'n' funky

As you grow taller and your body fills out, there will no doubt be times when you feel clumsy and at odds with yourself. After all, it's bound to take you a while to get used to your gorgeous new shape.

One thing that can really help is if you take up some form of regular exercise. If you already do exercise, you could try something new and more grown-up than you've done before. It can be fun to try yoga, aerobics, karate or salsa dancing, for instance. If you don't already exercise because you hate the kind of PE and Games you do at school, try something different. Exercise doesn't mean forcing yourself to do something you hate. There's a huge range of very different activities to choose from. So if you try out enough sports, you're bound to find something you really enjoy and which makes you feel good about your body. For instance, if you don't like team games, try something you can do on your own, such as swimming or line dancing or ice-skating. If you don't like being indoors, you could get together with your friends or family to go for a bike ride, a game of tennis, or a kick-about with a football in the park. If you like animals, you could ask a friend if you can walk her dog with her, or offer to help out at the local riding stables. Doing all these things will make you feel more in touch with your body and the way you move – so you'll feel confident and look confident too.

You'll notice as you grow up that you start to sweat more, especially when you exercise. So it's important to have a shower or bath every day and wash your sports kit after each wear. Don't forget to wear different socks each time you put on your trainers, either, or your feet will start smelling like stinky cheese!

It's also a good idea to use a deodorant spray or roll-on lotion just before you start racing about. You'll still get hot and damp, but it will keep you smelling sweet. Many girls like to use a deodorant every morning, to keep them fresh and fragrant through the day.

CHAPTER 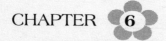 6

Be you!

Cool at school, happy at home

Growing-up is great because there are lots of exciting things to look forward to – parties and discos, falling in love with someone gorgeous, falling in love with someone even more gorgeous, going on holiday with your friends, and learning to drive. However, sometimes there might be disappointments too. The boy you've got your eye on might ignore you at a party. A couple of your friends might gang up together and leave you feeling left out. You might even find that learning to drive is harder than you thought. All these ups and downs can make you feel like you're on a rollercoaster. One minute, you're on top of the world – the next, you're right down in the dumps. The changes that happen to your body can do strange things to your feelings too. Even the sunniest girl in the world can start to be moody and feel really fed up with everything at times.

If you start to have these fantastic highs and not-so-fantastic lows, it doesn't mean that you're going mad, or that you're a nasty person, or that your life is no good. In fact, your friends will be feeling just the same way. It's a patch that everyone goes through. And these feelings won't last forever. As you get older, they will level out until you feel like your old self again. Hooray!

So if one day it seems like you've got out of bed on the wrong side, don't give yourself a hard time about feeling bad. As long as you're not nasty to people on purpose, it's OK not to be in a good mood with everybody *all* the time. Everybody is grumpy once in a while. It just can't be helped. So do something that you really enjoy, to cheer yourself up. Perhaps treat yourself to a luxurious bath and face pack, or tuck yourself away in your bedroom with your all-time favourite book.

And don't forget that your friends will sometimes feel the same. So if one of your mates has an off-day, it doesn't necessarily mean that you've done anything to upset her, or that she doesn't like you any more. You can bet that the blues will soon wear off and she'll be back to normal with you. In fact, you can help your friend through any rainy days by being especially kind and thoughtful to her. And of course, she'll be there to share all those fab good times with you, too.

HINTS FOR HAPPINESS

If you or your friends ever need cheering up, here are some great things that will stop you moping and start you smiling:

🌸 Show your best friend that you care by giving her a surprise present. Making her something is much more thoughtful than buying something. So why not plait her a friendship bracelet or make her a special card?

🌸 Treat your friend to a make-over. Ask your mums if she can stay the night and get some treats ready for her. Paint her fingers and toes with some nail art, stick on some sparkly body jewels, and think of a fab new way to do her hair that she couldn't manage by herself.

🌸 Think up something new that you and your friends will both enjoy doing together. For instance, suggest a club you could join or a new sport you could take up. Trying something different will really give you both a good giggle.

✿ Send your friends an email, e-card or
text message.

✿ Why not become pen-pals with your best
friend? After all, you don't have to live a long
way away from someone to send them a letter.
Put it in an envelope and address it – don't
forget a stamp – then pop it in the post. It will
really brighten up her day. She might even
send you one back …

✿ Get your friends round to watch one of your
favourite videos or DVDs.

Liking your friends

Having great friends is one of the very best things about being a girl. You go to the same school or the same clubs, and you're invited to the same parties. You like wearing the same fashions, having the same hairstyles, and listening to the same music. You like going out to the same places, doing the same things, reading the same books, and collecting the same stuff.

However, one of the most difficult things about growing up is that your life sometimes changes when you don't really want it to. You might find that you and your friends have to go to different secondary schools. As your bodies change shape, you might not look good wearing the same clothes any more. Your best friend might start growing boobs and having periods while there's no sign of yours arriving. All these things can come between you and your friends. So if some of your friends start making friends with other girls, it doesn't mean that they like you any less or that you're a nasty person. It just means that they're chumming up with someone whose life is changing more like their own than yours is. You can always keep in touch with them even if you're not able to meet up that often. You can ring for a chat, or send an email or text. If they're your true friends, they'll stay in touch. If they're not your true friends, then you're better off letting them go their own way. In any case, there will be plenty of other girls around who are desperate to be special friends with you. You might not have noticed before, because you've probably been too busy with your old friends. So keep smiling, just be yourself, and never join in with girls who say bad things about others, and you won't be on your own for very long.

Of course, many of your friends will stick with you through thick and thin, no matter what changes in your lives. Grown-ups often have lots of friends

they made when they were children, even though they've changed cities, jobs and boyfriends over the years. Your mum or auntie probably has great "girls' nights" when she gets together with her oldest, closest friends to chat and laugh and let their hair down having a good time.

However, it's only natural to make and break some friendships as you grow up. The most important thing is that you shouldn't try to change yourself just to fit in with a group. You don't have to wear the same clothes as someone or like the same popstars or say the same things to be their friend. If you can admire someone for being different, and they like you for being different too, you'll have a firm friendship that will grow stronger as you both grow up.

Girltalk

" Me, Tash, and Shaheena used to go round all the time as a three. We did everything together. Then Tash and Shaheena started doing things on their own. So I made friends with Jade. Now she's my best friend in all the world. It's much easier being a two than a three – no one's left out. "

Amrin from Manchester

Being with boys

At the moment you probably have one or two boys as friends. Although, some girls enjoy hanging around with boys more than with girls. Then again, perhaps you can't stand boys. On the other hand, you may already have a boyfriend... However you feel about boys at the moment, there will probably come a time when you meet a special one that makes your heart flip over. When this happens, you might find that you blush and get all shy and can't think of anything to say. Don't worry about it – this even happens to grown-ups. And one thing is for sure, if the boy likes you too, he'll be just as nervous as you.

Whether he's a popstar or just a boy in your class, you'll always come across a boy who makes you feel all giggly inside. But at the end of the day, boys are not special god-like beings from another planet. We're are all just *people.* There are a lot of fun ordinary things that girls and boys both like doing. For instance, athletics club, or orchestra, or being in a group that wants to save endangered animals. Joining an activity like this is a great way to meet gorgeous guys, and will guarantee that you and the object of your desire have got something in common to talk about, too. "Having a boyfriend" sounds quite important and official, but in fact it can just mean having a special boy that you enjoy doing activities like this with. It doesn't necessarily mean that you have to hold his hand or kiss him. If a boy tries to do something like put his arm around you and you don't want him to, just say, "Oh, I'm not really in the mood for that today, thanks," and move away. That way, you haven't hurt his feelings, but you haven't done anything you feel uncomfortable with either. Sorted.

Boy talk

Many girls find that a boy is totally different when he's on his own to when he's with a group of his mates. For instance, if you and your boyfriend are having tea at his house, he might be easy to talk to and have a laugh with. He might even say something really nice about how pretty you are. However, if your boyfriend is with his mates when you next see him, he might not even look you in the eye. How frustrating is that? Well, rest assured that your boyfriend probably hasn't gone off you. Boys tease each other about having girlfriends, just like some girls tease each other about having boyfriends. Your boyfriend just doesn't want to be wound up by his mates, that's all.

Then again, *everybody* gets dumped from time to time – even gorgeous models and popstars. If a boy tells you that he doesn't want you to be his girlfriend any more, it doesn't mean that you're not pretty or funny or lovely. You *are*. Your family still loves you and your friends still think you are great. In fact, your ex-boyfriend will probably still think you are gorgeous too. It's just that his eye has been caught by some other girl. After all, *you* have plenty more gorgeous boys to choose from, too. And many of them will be just dying to go out with you, without you realising it. So try not to feel too heartbroken. Instead of thinking about what's happened, enjoy spending time with your friends. Soon enough you'll get together with another boy. Then your friends will be complaining that you don't spend enough time with them any more ... It's a hard life being popular, isn't it?

Girltalk

66 I was 14 when I first got asked out. He was a boy I'd known for a long time at swimming club. I'd never really noticed that he was so good-looking before. At first, we both got really teased by our friends. But that was only 'cos they were all jealous. We split up a couple of months later but I've had loads of other boyfriends since then. 99

Katie from Leicester

Loving your family

Everybody has a family – your family is whoever you live with. All families are very different. In yours, you might have a mum, a dad, brothers and sisters, a gran or grandad, an auntie or uncle, foster-parents, or the other grown-ups and kids in a children's home. Some people with step-mums and step-dads have two families – or even three!

Whoever the people are in your family, they will be very proud of you as you grow up into a clever, kind, gorgeous adult. However, no matter how big you get, you will always be their little girl too. As you begin to want to do things without your family and with your friends instead, they might find it hard to "let go" of you. Your family will also be worried that something bad might happen to you while you are off doing things on your own. It's because your family cares about you so much that they will almost certainly want to lay down some rules about things like:

- where you can go on your own or with your friends and where you can't

- who you can go out with and who you should keep away from

- what clothes are cool to wear and when it's OK to try out make-up

- what time you should come home from places or what time they will pick you up

- how much time you should spend on your homework.

Sometimes you might feel some of these rules are tough and unfair. You may also start to disagree with your family's opinions on things. For instance, you might want to recycle stuff at home and they might not want to bother. You might want your step-dad to give up smoking and he might not be able to see the point. These kind of things can make you feel like getting really upset and shouting and stamping – but if you do, you really won't win.

Your family will think you're behaving childishly, so they won't pay you any attention. The cool thing to do is to talk calmly and honestly to your family about the way you feel. This way, they will start to see you as a grown-up and will listen to you much more. The most important thing of all is to *show* your family that you can take responsibility and behave sensibly. For instance, if you promise that you will be ready to leave a disco at a certain time, don't be late when your family or your friend's family come to pick you up. If you agree not to

wear lip-gloss to school, don't smuggle one into your schoolbag. When your family see that you can be trusted, they will let you do more and more things on your own. Result!

Families are fantastic for always being there if you need them to be. Remember that *all* families have little rows from time to time – and even big bust-ups – but this doesn't mean that people don't love and care for each other very much indeed. If you have any worries or problems, no matter how big or small, you should always talk to your family about them. That's what they're there for. Sometimes people find it easier to talk to a friend's family than to their own. That's absolutely fine – different families are better at some things than others. Remember, no matter how grown-up you are, there will always be people to love and look after you.

Don't worry, be happy

Starting periods, growing boobs, fighting spots, fancying boys, coping with boys fancying you – it can sound like a lot to handle, can't it? Well, don't worry. These things don't all happen at once. When you and your body are ready for periods, boobs and boyfriends, they'll come along over several years. You'll deal with them without realising and then you'll look back and wonder what all the fuss was about.

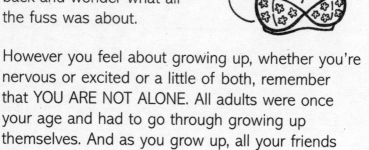

However you feel about growing up, whether you're nervous or excited or a little of both, remember that YOU ARE NOT ALONE. All adults were once your age and had to go through growing up themselves. And as you grow up, all your friends will grow up with you.

Finally, just because you're now all clued-up about growing up, it doesn't mean that you suddenly ARE a grown-up. You don't have to change in any way, whether it's giving up anything or starting to do anything new. No matter how old you are, you are still YOU, and being you is ALWAYS a very cool thing to be.

Now you've read this book you can give yourself ten out of ten for knowing all about periods. You might even be able to help answer some of your friends' questions about growing up. As you all turn into teenagers, you are going to share lots of great times together. Puberty is just the beginning of many fantastic things that lie ahead for you all. So start looking forward to lots of fun – and enjoy every minute of being a girl!

Helplines

Here are some numbers to ring if you need to talk to someone. They're all completely confidential (which means they're not allowed to tell anyone what you say) so you can pour your heart out.

Anti Bullying Campaign
Tel: 0207 378 1446

ChildLine
You can call for free at any time of the day or night and the number won't show up on the bill.
Tel: 0800 1111

AUSTRALIA
Kids Help Line
Telephone counselling service.
Tel: 1800 55 1800 (24 hours)

Lifeline
Confidential advice.
Tel: 13 11 14 (24 hours)

CANADA
Kids Help Phone
Tel: 1 800 668 6868 (24 hours)

NEW ZEALAND
Youthline
Tel: 0800 376 633

REPUBLIC OF IRELAND
ChildLine
Freephone 1800 666 666 (24 hours)

National Association for Victims of Bullying
Tel: 0506 31590

SOUTH AFRICA
ChildLine
Toll free 08000 55555 (24 hours)

Glossary

Check out the meanings of some of the words you've come across in this book and impress your friends with your knowledge.

amenorrhoea The word doctors and nurses use for if a girl's monthly periods stop, but she is not pregnant.

deodorant A perfumed spray or roll-on liquid to use every day under your arms to keep yourself fresh and sweet-smelling.

eggs Girls and women have tiny eggs the size of the tip of a needle inside their tummies. They are necessary for making babies. The medical name for an egg is an ovum.

flow The blood that comes out from between a girl's legs when she has a period. Your flow may last longer or shorter than another girl's, and the amount of blood may be more (heavier) or less (lighter) than another girl's.

irregular periods Many girls find they don't have the same number of days between periods. Some girls even skip a whole month or two without a period – particularly when their periods first start happening. This is called having irregular periods.

menstrual cycle The term doctors and nurses use for monthly periods. To work out the pattern of your own personal menstrual cycle see 'period pattern'.

mucus A small amount of liquid which might sometimes come out from between your legs. It might be clear, whitish or yellowish, and is perfectly normal and healthy.

ovaries Two little pods inside a girl's tummy which contain teeny-tiny eggs.

panty liner A very thin pad to stick inside your knickers when you think your period might be about to start, just in case.

period pad A specially-shaped pad to stick inside your knickers during your period, to soak up the blood.

period pain The aching a girl sometimes feels in her tummy and back on the first day or two of her period.

period pattern Another way of saying 'menstrual cycle' – or the number of days between your periods. You can work out your pattern on a calendar by marking the first day of each period as Day One, and then counting the days in between. See pages 48 and 49 to find out more.

pimple Another name for spots (see 'spots').

PMT (or PMS) A girl can feel grumpy or upset in the few days before her period – for no apparent reason. This is called PMT (or PMS). The letters stand for premenstrual tension (or premenstrual syndrome).

pregnant The term doctors and nurses use to describe when a woman has a baby growing inside her tummy.

puberty The years in your life when your body makes grown-up changes, such as growing boobs and starting periods. Puberty usually begins any time between nine and 17 years old.

sanitary towels All kinds of period pads and panty liners. The term 'sanitary protection' means tampons too.

sex 'Having sex' or 'making love' is when a man and woman share a special cuddle which can result in them having a baby. For ways to find out more, see pages 54–59.

sperm Boys and men make inside their bodies teeny-tiny things shaped rather like tadpoles, called sperm. Sperm is necessary for making babies.

spots Greasy lumps that can appear on your skin after the age of about nine – particularly on your face, back or chest. There are lots of names for spots, including pimples, zits, blackheads and whiteheads.

tampon A tampon is a type of period pad made specially to be worn inside your body, where the blood comes out. It looks like a roll of cotton wool about the size of a lipstick. It has a string attached, so you can pull it out easily when you want to change it.

teenagers Girls and boys are called teenagers when they are between the ages of around 13 to 18.

tubes Girls and women have two tubes inside their tummies which boys and men don't have. These play a part in having periods and in making babies. The full name is Fallopian tubes.

vagina The passageway in a girl or woman's body through which period blood flows out and through which babies are born.

womb The space inside a woman where a baby grows. The word doctors and nurses use for womb is 'uterus'.

Index